First published in Great Britain by HarperCollins Children's Books in 2004
3 5 7 9 10 8 6 4 2
ISBN: 0-00-717165-X
Text © 2004 HarperCollinsPublishers Ltd
Bang on the door character copyright:
© 2004 Bang on the Door all rights reserved.
bang on the door is a trademark
Exclusive right to license by Santoro
www.bangonthedoor.com
A CIP catalogue record for this title is available from the British Library.
No part of this publication may be reproduced, stored in a retrieval system or transmitted in
any form or by any means, electronic, mechanical, photocopying, recording or otherwise, with-
out the prior permission of HarperCollinsPublishers Ltd, 77-85 Fulham Palace Road,
Hammersmith, London W6 8JB. The HarperCollins website address is:
www.harpercollins.co.uk
All rights reserved.
Printed and bound in Hong Kong

bang on the door™ ©

football crazy's big match

Collins

An imprint of HarperCollinsPublishers

Meet **football crazy**! He is just mad about football! He has been dreaming of winning the cup final for so long. Now the big day is finally here. Will his dream come true?

What is **football crazy**'s team called?

Football is played all over the world!

There's a lot to do before the big match.
First, **football crazy** gets his kit ready.

↑ football crazy's
favourite player!

← 5 hours until kick off!

practice ball
to warm up with

favourite pair of boots

football shorts

football shirt

oranges for half-time

extra pair of boots
with 'moulded' studs for hard ground

water bottles

football socks

spare whistle
incase the referee forgets his!

camera for a team photo!

shower gel

for after the game!

⚽ How many things are in football crazy's kit?
⚽ Football boots have studs on the bottom to
help stop you slipping on the pitch.

On the way to the match **football crazy** thinks about scoring the winning goal and practises a few kicks in the park.

⚽ What colour are **football crazy's** boots?
⚽ Big matches are played in stadiums with thousands of fans watching, but you could play a game with your friends at the park.

At last it's nearly time for the big match to begin.

⚽ **Football crazy** has forgotten something very important. Can you see what it is?

⚽ A full game lasts 90 minutes and is split into two halves — the 'first half' and the 'second half'. Each 'half' is 45 minutes long.

Just before the match starts, the players warm up. They run up and down the pitch and stretch their arms and legs.

It is important to warm up and stretch your muscles before a game.

stretch

swing

bend

lift

Football crazy practises passing the ball.

The players kick with the insides of their feet.

Sometimes **football crazy** uses the outside of his foot to shoot at the goal!

⚽ How many players are warming up?
⚽ Passing the ball means kicking it to another player.

All the players start the game in their own position. **Football crazy** is playing centre forward.

football crazy

team mate

team mates

team mate

- There are 22 players plus the referee! Substitutes wait on the benches — they might get to play later in the game.
- How many goalkeepers are there?
- The referee makes sure the game is fair and nobody breaks the rules!

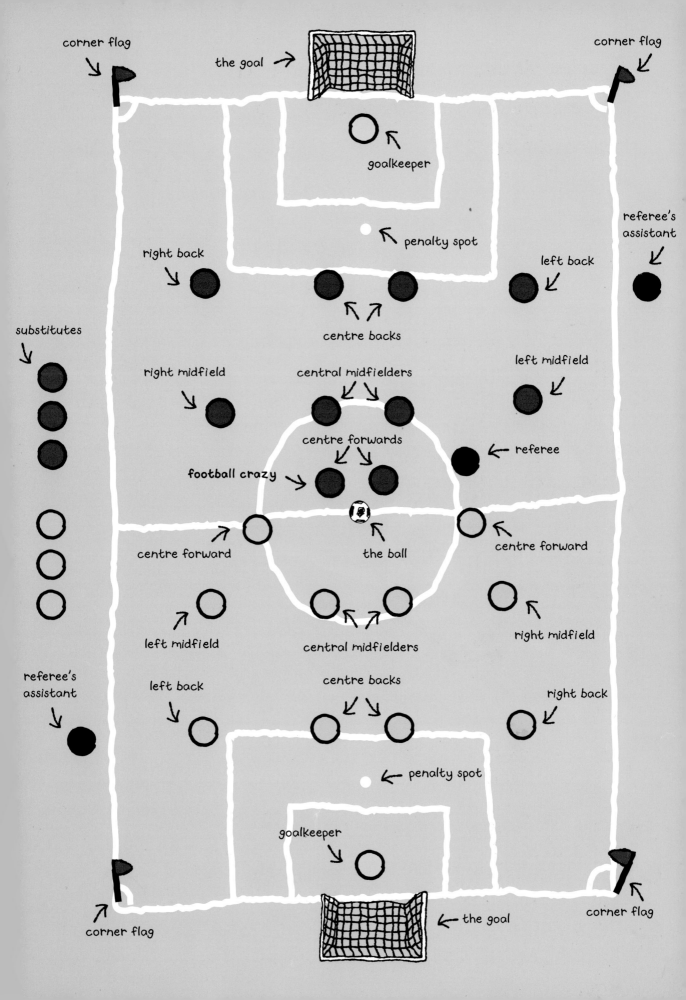

The referee tosses a coin to decide which team will kick off. Oh, dear — **football crazy's** team loses the toss!

kick off!

The ball has to be kicked forwards to start the match.

- If a player breaks the rules the referee can give a yellow card as a warning!
- Except for throw ins, only the goalkeepers and the referee are allowed to touch the ball with their hands.

corner kick!

A corner is awarded when a player kicks the ball off the field behind his own goal line.

throw in!

The ball must go behind your head before you take a throw in.

free kick!

The defenders must be 10 yards away from where the free kick is taken.

Football crazy has the ball but **disaster**, a player tackles him and the other team scores!

Tackling is using your feet to take the ball away from a player for the other team!

Who is blowing the whistle?

good shot!

goal!

great tackle!

Just then, the whistle blows. It's half-time and football **crazy**'s team are losing the game!

At half-time the team talks about
the game and how they can win.

tactics board

They eat oranges for energy and drink lots of water. **Football crazy** is very thirsty after all the running around.

⚽ Can you find **football crazy**'s water bottle?

⚽ Either team can substitute up to 3 players during the game — a substitute player takes their place!

As the second half kicks off the other team scores again! What now?

Then something happens — it turns out the goal is not allowed because one of the other team's players is offside!

Offside!

A player is offside if he is nearer to the other team's goal line than the ball and all but one of the other team's players.

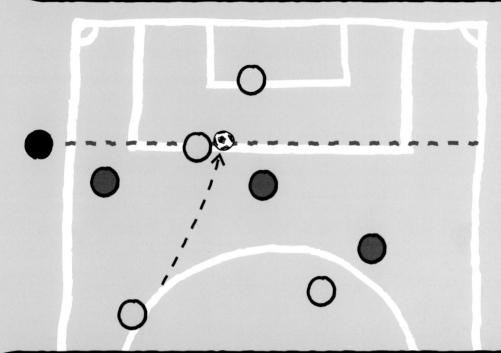

Not offside!

A player is not in an offside position if he is in his own side of the pitch, he is level with the second last player from the other team or he is level with the last two players from the other team.

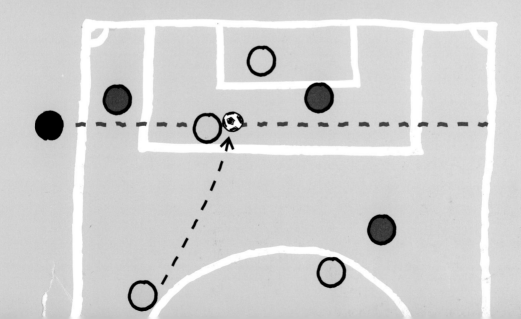

Football crazy still wants to win the game. He quickly dribbles the ball past all the other players. He can see the goal! Then... Ouch! Landing in a painful heap on the grass, **football crazy** rubs his sore knees and elbows. Poor **football crazy**. He's been fouled!

Action replay:
Ouch!

- ⚽ Dribbling the ball means kicking it along and running at the same time. It takes lots of practise to get really good!
- ⚽ Getting a red card means a player has broken the rules and is not allowed to play!

The referee shows a
red card and sends the
other player off.

red card!

Now **football crazy** has
a chance to score — the
referee awards him a penalty!
Football crazy lines up, steps back and **thwack**,
he kicks the ball straight past the goalie and into
the back of the net. Hooray!

penalty!
goal!!

penalty spot

Now **football crazy**'s team have a chance to win the match after all! **Football crazy**'s boots are a blur as he runs all over the pitch!

he beats one!

great volley!

he beats two!

fab dribbling!

he beats three!

bad tackle!

super skills!

At the last minute he shoots and scores another **goal!**

What is the final score?

The final whistle blows — they've won the cup!

All the players shake hands after the game.

The winning team get to keep the cup until the next final!

Hooray! football crazy's
big match dream
has come true!

Collect 5 tokens and get a free poster!*

All you have to do is collect five funky tokens!
You can snip one from any of these cool Bang on the Door books!

bang on the door
ballet girl goes shopping

0 00 715297 3

bang on the door
little princess joins in

0 00 715309 0

bang on the door
little madam's party

0 00 715307 4

bang on the door
little sweetheart dresses up

0 00 715308 2

bang on the door
super hero boy's activity book

world-saving puzzles and hero-tastic things to do!

0 00 715313 9

Send 5 tokens with a completed coupon to:
Bang on the Door Poster Offer

PO Box 142, Horsham, RH13 5FJ
(UK residents)

c/- HarperCollins Publishers (NZ) Ltd,
PO Box 1, Auckland
(NZ residents)

c/- HarperCollins Publishers,
PO Box 321, Pymble NSW 2073, Australia
(Australian residents)

bang on the door
groovy chick activity book

fab 'n' funky puzzles and groovy things to do!

0 00 717635 X

bang on the door
football crazy's activity book

footie fun with top-scoring puzzles and things to do!

0 00 716983 3

0 00 715306 6

bang on the door
the groovy picnic surprise

0 00 715305 8

bang on the door
the cool sleepover secret

bang on the door
ballet girl's activity book

twirly girly puzzles and tutu-tastic things to do!

0 00 715312 0

✂

Title: Mr ☐ Mrs ☐ Miss ☐ Ms ☐ First name: .... Surname: ....

Address: ....

....

Postcode: .... Child's date of birth: ..... / ..... /

email address: ....

Signature of parent/guardian: ....

Tick here if you wish to receive further information about children's books ☐

Terms and Conditions: Proof of sending cannot be considered proof of receipt. Not redeemable for cash. Please allow 28 days for delivery.
Photocopied tokens not accepted. Offer open to UK, New Zealand and Australia residents only while stocks last. *rrp £3.99

FC02

1 token